I Like Sports Stars!

Read About Drew Brees

David P. Torsiello

Enslow Elementary
an imprint of
Enslow Publishers, Inc.
40 Industrial Road
Box 398
Berkeley Heights, NJ 07922
USA
http://www.enslow.com

For Ms. DiPiazza:
Your dedication to teaching is what dedicated me to learning.

Enslow Elementary, an imprint of Enslow Publishers, Inc.
Enslow Elementary® is a registered trademark of Enslow Publishers, Inc.

Library of Congress Cataloging-in-Publication Data

Torsiello, David P.
Read about Drew Brees / David P. Torsiello.
p. cm. — (I like sports stars!)
Includes bibliographical references and index.
Summary: "Drew Brees is the quarterback for the New Orleans Saints. In addition to being one of the top quarterbacks in the game, Drew Brees has also done a great deal to help the people of New Orleans recover from the devastation of Hurricane Katrina"—Provided by publisher.
ISBN 978-0-7660-3831-8
1. Brees, Drew, 1979—Juvenile literature. 2. Football players—United States—Biography—Juvenile literature. 3. New Orleans Saints (Football team)—Juvenile literature. I. Title.
GV939.B695T67 2011
796.332092--dc23
[B] 2011020412

Papberback ISBN: 978-1-59845-299-0

Printed in the United States of America

062011 Lake Book Manufacturing, Inc., Melrose Park, IL

10 9 8 7 6 5 4 3 2 1

Enslow Publishers, Inc., is committed to printing our books on recycled paper. The paper in every book contains 10% to 30% post-consumer waste (PCW). The cover board on the outside of each book contains 100% PCW. Our goal is to do our part to help young people and the environment too!

To Our Readers: We have done our best to make sure all Internet Addresses in this book were active and appropriate when we went to press. However, the author and the publisher have no control over and assume no liability for the material available on those Internet sites or on links to other Web sites. Any comments or suggestions can be sent by e-mail to comments@enslow.com or to the address on the back cover.

Every effort has been made to locate all copyright holders of material used in this book. If any errors or omissions have occurred, corrections will be made in future editions of this book.

Photo Credits: AP Images/Al Behrman, p. 14; AP Images/Ann Heisenfelt, pp. 13, 15; AP Images/Bill Haber, pp. 16, 17; AP Images/Scott Boehm, pp. 18-19; Jed Jacobsohn/Getty Images, p. 21; AP Images/David Stluka, pp. 20, 22, 23; AP Images/Denis Poroy, pp. 8, 9; AP Images/Ed Zurga, p. 12; AP Images/Eric Gay, p. 7; Rick Stewart/Getty Images, p. 11; AP Images/Lenny Ignelzi, p. 4; AP Images/Mark Humphrey, pp. 1, 10; AP Images/Michael Conroy, p. 6;

Cover Photo: AP Images/Mark Humphrey

Contents

Words to Know

draft—How football teams select players out of college.

hurricane—A big storm with very strong wind.

pass—A throw from a quarterback in football.

quarterback—The player who throws the ball. Sometimes he hands the ball to another player who will run with it.

Super Bowl—The championship game of football.

touchdown—A score in football when a player reaches the end zone with the ball.

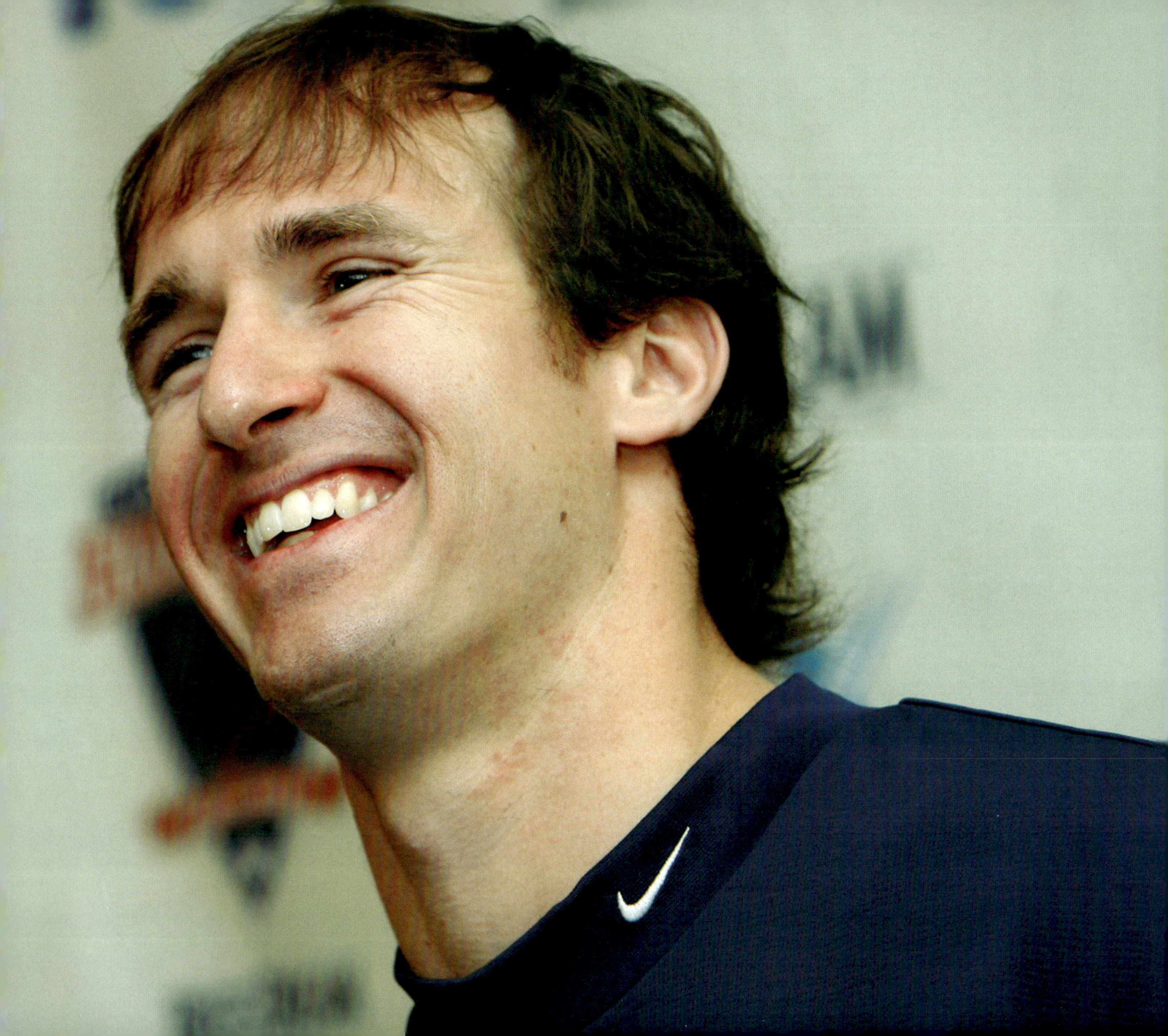

Drew Brees was born on January 15, 1979.
He plays quarterback for the New Orleans
Saints.

Drew Brees played college football for Purdue University. He played very well in college.

ALAMO
BOWL
15

Riddell
9

After college, the San Diego Chargers drafted Drew. He played in San Diego for five years.

Riddell
SAINTS
9
25

In 2006, Drew Brees became quarterback for the New Orleans Saints. Drew was happy to be in New Orleans.

The Saints started winning with Drew on the team. Drew threw many touchdown passes. The Saints also got better at running the ball.

Riddell

Drew's passing got better each season.

He would even run with the ball when he had to. Drew would do anything to win a game!

The year before Drew joined the Saints, Hurricane Katrina struck New Orleans. Drew worked hard to help rebuild the city.

In 2010, Drew Brees led the Saints all the way to the Super Bowl! The Saints played the Indianapolis Colts. The Colts were also a great team.

Riddell
SUPER BOWL

Drew Brees led the Saints to a Super Bowl victory with two touchdown passes!

SAINTS
9

Drew Brees held up the Super Bowl trophy after the game was over. The Saints were champions for the first time!

Further Reading

Portman, Michael. *Drew Brees.* New York: Gareth Stevens, 2010.

Savage, Jeff. *Drew Brees.* Minneapolis: Lerner Publications, 2011.

Internet Address

Drew Brees, QB for the New Orleans Saints at NFL.com

http://www.nfl.com/players/drewbrees/profile?id=BRE229498

Index